Finding Lucy

eugenie fernandes

pajamapress

First published in Canada and the United States in 2019

 Canada Council   Conseil des arts
for the Arts   du Canada

 ONTARIO ARTS COUNCIL
CONSEIL DES ARTS DE L'ONTARIO
an Ontario government agency
un organisme du gouvernement de l'Ontario

Canadä

The publisher gratefully acknowledges the support of the Canada Council for the Arts and the Ontario Arts Council for its publishing program. We acknowledge the financial support of the Government of Canada through the Canada Book Fund (CBF) for our publishing activities.

Library and Archives Canada Cataloguing in Publication

Title: Finding Lucy / by Eugenie Fernandes.
Names: Fernandes, Eugenie, 1943- author.
Identifiers: Canadiana 20190086939 | ISBN 9781772780888 (softcover)
Classification: LCC PS8561.E7596 F56 2019 | DDC jC813/.54—dc23

Publisher Cataloging-in-Publication Data (U.S.)

Names: Fernandes, Eugenie, 1943-, author, illustrator.
Title: Finding Lucy / by Eugenie Fernades.
Description: Toronto, Ontario Canada : Pajama Press, 2019. | Summary: "Lucy is happy painting the color of laughter in her garden, but loses her way when she follows feedback from a series of animal critics. With wise encouragement from her cat, Lucy finds her authentic self in her work again and painting is rewarding once more"— Provided by publisher.
Identifiers: ISBN 978-1-77278-088-8 (hardcover)
Subjects: LCSH: Creation (Literary, artistic, etc.) – Juvenile fiction. | Criticism – Juvenile fiction. | Encouragement – Juvenile fiction. | BISAC: JUVENILE FICTION / Art. | JUVENILE FICTION / Animals / General. | JUVENILE FICTION / Social Themes / Emotions & Feelings.
Classification: LCC PZ7.F476Fin |DDC [E] – dc23

Original art created with acrylic paint on canvas.
Cover and book design—Rebecca Bender

Manufactured by Qualibre Inc. / Printplus
Printed in China

Pajama Press Inc.
181 Carlaw Ave. Suite 251 Toronto, Ontario Canada, M4M 2S1

Distributed in Canada by UTP Distribution
5201 Dufferin Street Toronto, Ontario Canada, M3H 5T8

Distributed in the U.S. by Ingram Publisher Services
1 Ingram Blvd. La Vergne, TN 37086, USA

For **Robyn**,
of course,
    and for **Ellee**,
     and for
      Troon

When Lucy took her paints
outside to the garden,
the cat purred,
and Lucy painted,
and Lucy was happy,
until, one day...

...a reporter came from the *Daily News.* "What are you doing?" asked the reporter.

"I am painting the color of laughter," said Lucy.

"That's ridiculous," said the reporter. "It looks like JELLYBEAN SOUP!"

The cat bristled. His whiskers twitched.

"Jellybean soup?" said Lucy.

After reading the reporter's report, the curious got curious. An elephant came to listen to the color—but she could not hear the laughter.

"It's as quiet as a mouse," she said. "It isn't LOUD enough."

"I will try to make it louder," said Lucy, and she offered the elephant tea.

After the elephant tea...

...a crocodile came to EAT the art.

He thought it would taste like jellybean soup.

But, "CHOMP-CHOMP-UGH!" he said. "This is disgusting! It isn't SCRUMPTIOUS enough."

"I will try to make it more scrumptious," said Lucy.

The crocodile grinned a magnificent grin.

Then the elephant
and the crocodile
sailed away to see
the wide, wide world.

The cat was not unhappy
to see them go.

Lucy took a deep breath.

And then she started
to paint again, and the
painting was like a dream.

But then...

...a chicken came blustering down the lane. "This painting isn't BRAVE enough," thundered the chicken.

"I am *sure* it *will* get braver," said Lucy firmly.

"It will never be braver than ME," said the chicken.

All of a sudden, the chicken jumped over the moon, and where she came down, nobody knows.

"PINK!" shouted the mother pig. "There's not enough PINK! My babies cannot SLEEP without PINK!"

So Lucy added pink— lots of pink.

She painted a lullaby of pink, and the babies fell asleep... and that was a big relief.

But now, of course, there was TOO MUCH PINK!

"I think you need some green," whispered the frog.

"Maybe so," sighed Lucy— and she poured a whole bucket of green all over the painting.

"That's better," said the frog.

"Better is better," said Lucy, and then she kissed the frog— and when she did...

...the frog began to sing.

"HOLY POLLYWOG!" cried Lucy.
"You have a beautiful voice. Why...
you could sing on Broadway."

"That's a long way to hop," said
the frog, "but I would like to try."

"You can do it," said Lucy.

"I *can* do it," said the frog.

So he did—
and now he is singing
on Broadway.

By now, Lucy was beginning to see that *everybody* had *something* to say.

She heard them mutter, "It's utterly befuddling and baffling and piffling and dribbling and scribbling!"

"Never mind that," said the cat.

At last, the big-city critic arrived. He took one look and shook his head. "It's much too beautiful," he said. "It isn't FEROCIOUS enough."

Lucy wobbled. She did *not* want to change the painting, however, she *did* want to please the big-city critic. So Lucy splattered the beautiful painting with ink and garbage and mud.

"E-GADS!" cried the critic. "This is ATROCIOUS!"

And off he went in a babble of flabbergasting words.

Lucy was all
DIS–COM–BOB–U–LATED.
A gloomy silence fell over the garden.

"I can remember," said the cat, "when you were painting the warmness of yellow."

"And the melody of tangerine," said Lucy, "and the poetry of blue. I miss that."

"Me too," said the cat.

Right then and there, Lucy got busy.

She painted the flutter of birds and the whimsy of the wind.

"You might find this hard to believe," she said, "but I'm starting to feel like myself again."

"That's FAN-TAB-U-LOUS," said the cat.

"How lucky I am," said Lucy, "to have a friend like you."

And ever after, after that,
the cat purred,
and Lucy painted with grit
and determination
and GUMPTION
and PIZZAZZ.

And the courage of spring
and the color of laughter.